T0171221

GOD'S PLAN

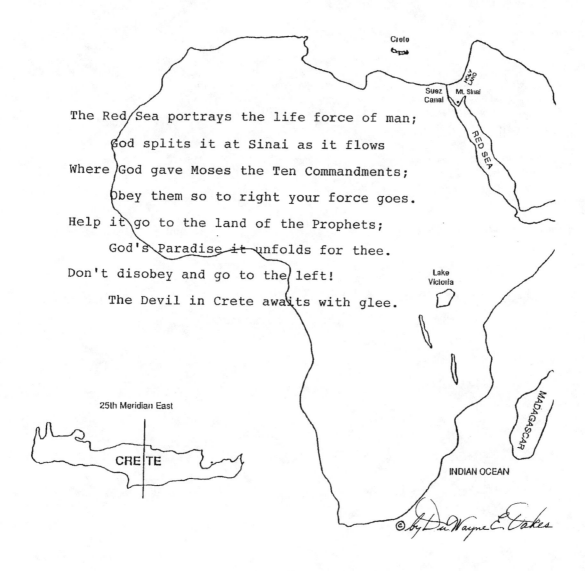

The Red Sea portrays the life force of man;
    God splits it at Sinai as it flows
Where God gave Moses the Ten Commandments;
    Obey them so to right your force goes.
Help it go to the land of the Prophets;
    God's Paradise it unfolds for thee.
Don't disobey and go to the left!
    The Devil in Crete awaits with glee.

DuWayne E. Oakes

Bloomington, IN   authorHOUSE®   Milton Keynes, UK

AuthorHouse™
1663 Liberty Drive, Suite 200
Bloomington, IN 47403
www.authorhouse.com
Phone: 1-800-839-8640

© 2006 DuWayne E. Oakes. All Rights Reserved.

No part of this book may be reproduced, stored in a retrieval system, or transmitted by any means without the written permission of the author.

First published by AuthorHouse 07/1/09

ISBN: 978-1-4259-0799-0 (e)
ISBN: 978-1-4259-0801-0 (sc)

Printed in the United States of America
Bloomington, Indiana

This book is printed on acid-free paper.

GOD'S PLAN

Through the earth's Godhead
God calls you to commune with him

God's objective proof of Jesus as the Godhead,
his presence and desires.

by
DuWayne E. Oakes
Copyright June 4, 1999,
and July 17, 2002

Leaders of the world rejoice;
    You see God's Plan for you.
Earth's Judgment has been planned by God;
    For all to see his view.

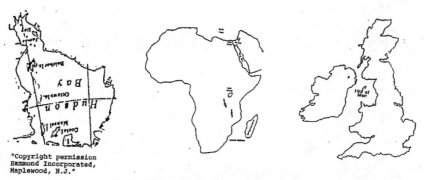

"Copyright permission
Hammond Incorporated,
Maplewood, N.J."

A PEEK AT GOD'S SIGNS

The Bible bold in thoughts foretold,
    God's Spirit in the waters lay.
So take a map, and look and see,
    His form in James and Hudson Bay.

Christ cried and reigns for God and man,
    To give Communion for our day.
A look at Africa will reveal
    God formed his head and bread, the way.

God's bread's a foot for you to wear -
    To church, this message to be told.
His love for you will always be,
    The reason for this message bold.

God's Spirit as a dove it came,
    When John baptized God's son.
In Ireland's form, it is the same.
    To Isle of Man, you see it come.

Now you see what God has planned,
    The Father, Son, and Holy Ghost.
Spread this word for all to know,
    That Earth confirms the way to go.

So be baptized in God's own water,
    And pledge your life to him.
The Ten Commandments he says obey;
    And follow Christ, for he's the way.

*   Poem in International Poetry Hall of Fame Museum

JESUS THE WAY

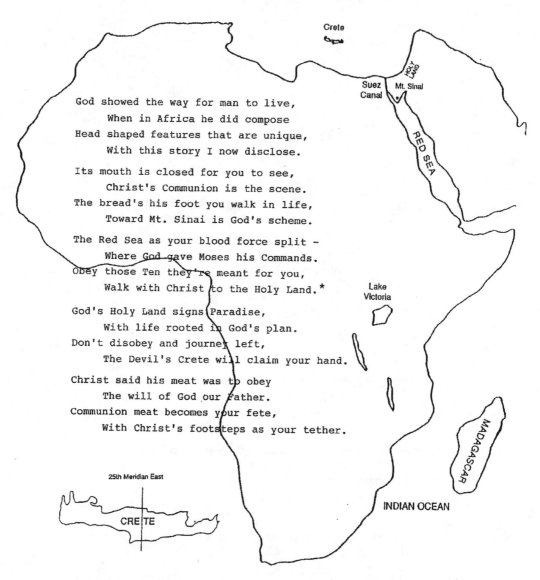

God showed the way for man to live,
    When in Africa he did compose
Head shaped features that are unique,
    With this story I now disclose.

Its mouth is closed for you to see,
    Christ's Communion is the scene.
The bread's his foot you walk in life,
    Toward Mt. Sinai is God's scheme.

The Red Sea as your blood force split –
    Where God gave Moses his Commands.
Obey those Ten they're meant for you,
    Walk with Christ to the Holy Land.*

God's Holy Land signs Paradise,
    With life rooted in God's plan.
Don't disobey and journey left,
    The Devil's Crete will claim your hand.

Christ said his meat was to obey
    The will of God our Father.
Communion meat becomes your fete,
    With Christ's footsteps as your tether.

*   Joshua, meaning Jesus, crossed over into the Holy Land.
    Poem in International Poetry Hall of Fame Museum.

The Ten Commmandments should be a fad;
    To warm your heart and make you glad.
So learn these Ten and take a stand;
    'Walk' with Christ to the Holy Land.

THE TEN COMMANDMENTS IN BRIEF

The Lord is my God.
I will not worship any engraved image.
I will not take the Lord's name in vain.
I will remember to keep Sunday holy.
I will honor my father and mother.
I will not kill, commit adultery, steal,
    bear false witness or covet.

WHY I WROTE

When I was a young man attending Concordia Lutheran College in Moorhead, Minnesota, I was beckoned to by a Light that was about the size of a man, in the upper right branches of a large evergreen tree. The Bible says that God is Light, and I have come to call that evergreen tree a grown up Christ Tree. This happened in the Spring of 1950, when I was walking home from class one afternoon. The Light was in a southeasterly direction, away from the sun. I was walking North from it when an unseen presence penetrated my being. It consumed my inner soul and caused me to wither before it. I turned and was enthralled, consumed by a glorious feeling of respectful Love. I continued to feel the beckoning it imparted to me, even as I walked away. It haunted me! The Bible also says that God is Love. (I John 4:8). At various times throughout the 1950's I came to have that same feeling of intense love when I would have Communion from Pastor Laverne Nelsen, at Bethlehem Lutheran Church in Tacoma, Washington. I next experienced that feeling of love when Pastor Ed Nesse visited my home in 1972 and gave me Communion.

After Pastor Nesse gave me Communion in my home, I had an urge one day to look at my Encyclopaedia Britannica Atlas. I took it downstairs, sat down, and it opened up-side-down to the map of North America. As it did so, I recognized the characterization of my Grandmother Annie Anderson sitting in her rocking chair in James and Hudson Bays, and that same feeling of Love entered my being. I next flipped the atlas right side up, and it opened to the map of the continent of Africa. I immediately saw God's message of Holy Christian Communion. After thinking of God's Spirit being in the waters when he formed the earth, I knew God used Grandma to communicate his message of Holy Christian Communion. I was so obsessed with God's summoning love, that for a long time I sought out meanings on maps for messages from him. It was not until I thought about my father's English and Irish heritage that I looked at the map of the British Isles, and made the analogy of the Holy Spirit coming to 'The Isle of Man'. When I thought about my mother's Scandinavian heritage, I made the analogy of Denmark appearing as Saint Peter in the shape of a hooded Spirit, holding the keys to the kingdom of heaven, represented as Gotland, meaning Godland. The keys were given to him by Jesus Christ. (Matthew 16:13-20). God knew that a picture is worth 10,000 words. Later, I was awakened one night and a Spirit form of Light similar in shape to Ireland encompassed and wrestled my body, similar to what happened to Jacob. (Gen. 32:24). I was later awakened and my face was breathed on. Jesus breathed on his disciples after he was resurrected, telling them to receive the Holy Ghost. (John 20:22).

When Abraham journeyed to Canaan, and came to the Oak of Moreh (Genesis 12:6), God promised to give his seed what came to be called the Holy Land. Abraham, which means the Father is High, then built the first altar to God at the Oak of Moreh, which means Oak of the Teacher. It was a teacher that this Oak, DuWayne became. And through me, DuWayne Oakes, God has now summarized his call for Communion with Christ. My writings are basically an extension of Christ's Light because of how it affected me.

As Light from a Christ Tree
    God beckoned to me like Saul.
I withered there in obeisance
    As his Love consumed my all.

God caused me to prove his coming;
    And when I tried to tell,
That minister would not believe me;
    So I vowed to write it well.

"Copyright permission Hammond Incorporated. Maplewood, N. J."

GOD'S EYE OF COMMUNION

God the King watches over me;
        As shown in James and Hudson Bays.
His 'eye' attends where I have lived,
        And write his plan to rule man's days.

Christ appeared to Paul as Light,
        And to me from in a Christ Tree.
He beckoned me to him as Light;
        Consumed my inner soul for thee.

And when Communion I did have
        'Twas like his Spirit that I swallowed.
And then again when I saw God
        In James and Hudson Bay it followed.

My head is shown upon that shore;
        The Nelson* and Mattagami frame it.
The Lord cut in when Reverend Nelsen
        Gave me Communion for to refit.

See eye of God the Communion Bread;
        His inner Body's Light came in.*
'Eat' from the Book of James our deed;
        Christ's brother's thoughts of God to win.

Akimiski Isle is Communion Bread.
        Land Across is what it means.
Godland is that Land Across;
        Where angels go to live on greens.

* Nelson and Nelsen both mean Son of the Champion.
  The 'Communion Eye' is the light of the body.
  Akimiski Isle is noted in McMillan Book of
  Canadian Place Names, by William Hamilton. It
  was first called Viner's Isle.

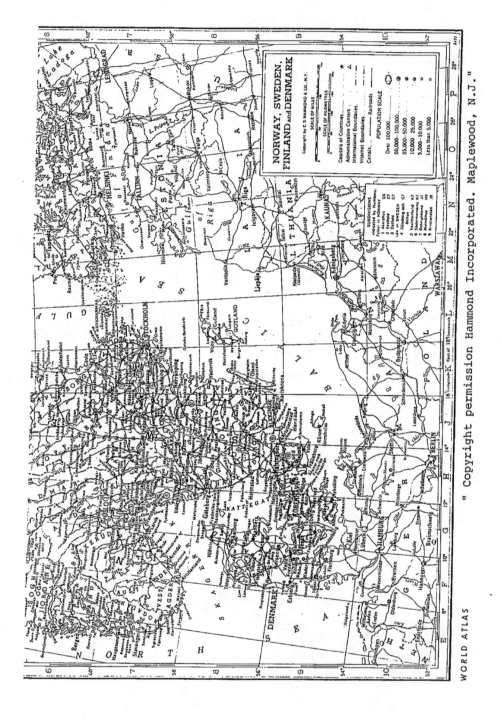

NORWAY, SWEDEN,
FINLAND and DENMARK

Copyright by C.S. HAMMOND & CO. N.Y.

SCALE OF MILES

SCALE OF KILOMETRES

Capitals of Countries.............. ★
Administrative Centers............. ▲
International Boundaries...........
Internal Boundaries...............
Canals..............Railroads......

POPULATION SCALE

Over 100,000.........
50,000-100,000.......
25,000-50,000........
10,000-25,000........
5,000-10,000.........
Less than 5,000......

SUBDIVISIONS
indicated by Numbers:
Fylker in NORWAY
1 Akershus   G6
2 Vestfold   G7
3 Oslofjord   G7
Län in SWEDEN
4 Göteborg och   G7
  Bohus
5 Västmanland   K7
6 Södermanland   K7
7 Örebro   J7
8 Malmöhus   H9
9 Kristianstad   J8

WORLD ATLAS   " Copyright permission Hammond Incorporated. Maplewood, N.J. "

10

PETER'S DEPICTED IN DENMARK

Jesus called Peter the Rock -
    He would build his church on him.
Then gave him the keys to heaven,
    To meet us as life closes in.

Denmark stands as a hooded knight,
    Peter with keys in his hand,
Guarding the Bold Sea to Godland*;
    Where Wise Village and Rome are clanned.

Estonia looks apprehensive;
    As a 'dog' it's shaped in land.
Dogs have been called unbelievers;
    Yet they eat from their master's hand.

The Pope is the Vicar of Christ;
    Peter still guards his stand.
As Christians we see it's meant
    Time's come to join the Pope's Band.

* Baltic means Bold. Gotland means
Godland. Visby meaning Wise Village is
the capital, and Roma is its closest
prominent city.

11

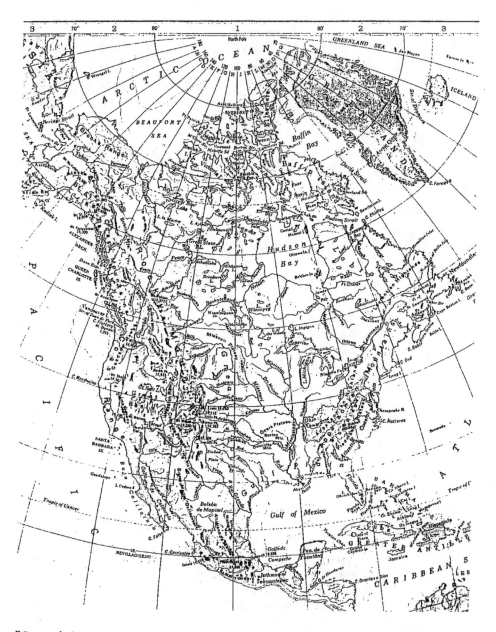

"Copyright permission Hammond Incorporated. Maplewood, N. J."

EAT FROM THE BOOK OF JAMES

Eat the Lord's Supper with God;
    Join in his mold in Canada.
God's form shapes head on southwestern shore.
    This mouth isn't closed like Africa.

As you eat from the Book of James,
    The Severn River flows from your mind;
Severn meaning extent or limit
    Of God's stomach's acquiring bind.

Severn flows to Hooded One's Son,
    As Peter with keys in his hand;
Judging those to stay with God.
    With Brother James, Christ shows his stand.

'Tis said that to chin means to talk.
    St. Joseph was Christ's Father's name.
The Albany starts at St. Joseph Lake;
    Christ's 'Father' did talk to James.

The mind that eats from the Book of James
    Flows into the 'stomach' of God;
To Hudson, meaning Hooded One's Son,
    With God's key for a heavenly nod.

I know the son of a Danish 'knight'.
    The King of Denmark he guarded.
Carl Fynboe is the son God signed;
    Through Peter and God he's regarded.

Saved spirits flow out of Hooded Son's Strait
    To Peter's Denmark with Safe Harbor.
On to 'Godland', God's own heaven;
    To live with Christ forever more.

"Copyright permission Hammond Incorporated, Maplewood, N.J."

AN ODE TO LEFTIES

God's left hand is in America;
    He made its form in Michigan State.
God our King, our heavenly Pa,
    Set his Paw in Michigan's shape.

Michigan means a really Big Lake;
    A Superior Lake for you to see
God's fluid form for life we take;
    Of James and Hudson Bays for free.

Lake Huron also frames that Paw.
    A bristle head is Huron's meaning.
James Bay is where you see it.
    God bristles that you learn his leaning.

God as a lefty, his form you see,
    When you look at James and Hudson Bays.
His Spirit does shape our destiny;
    Reeling in water he forms our ways.

A lefty's concern is social care;
    Sharing in life to free us from strife.
Giving this word so all may share;
    Caring that all may have a good life.

Put God first as the savior of men.
    Material worship will ruin it all.
God's shown his left, so think of him.
    Christ is our mentor, follow his call.

See Knight of Denmark as he stands;
    The likeness of Peter with God's keys
To God's Safe Harbor in his hands;
    So souls are reborn as he forsees.

CHRIST THE SOCIALIST

Christ told the disciples twelve
    To live with all things in common.
So did the first members dwell;
    In his church that now lives on.

As time progressed they changed,
    And God's message to others spread.
O'er all the world it ranged;
    That all be cared for and fed.

Christ a Socialist in his life;
    His faith in man now judging
Our love and giving to end all strife
    Of God's creations while ranging.

Humane birth control we do need;
    Cause resources limit man's span.
It's best to limit the people
    Than watch them starve with no plan.

Christian democracies through concern
    Are in vogue with rights and care.
Combine them with social programs;
    Christ's wish for life that is fair.

Isle of
Man

ENGLES AS ANGEL

In the Preface of the First Edition
     Of Das Kapital Engles wrote
The Thoughts of Marx on legal change.
     For England, he was found to quote.

He lived in England and decided
     It should have peaceful, legal change;
Its social economic evolution
     So advanced he would not disarrange.

Most countries are now so developed
     They surpass what England had then.
So Engles, meaning Angels, expressed
     God's thoughts of peace for all men.

If you are an Engles 'angel',
     And believe in Christ's Godly way,
Go forth as an 'angel' of Christ;
     Drawing others to churchly sway.

WHAT'S FAIR

You do it unto me -
        As you do it to the least.
'Twas said for all by Jesus;
        That we may join his feast.

Inner city unemployment
        Is thirty percent all toll.
One third of young black men
        Are in jail, probation or parol.

Break return to prison life!
        Turn our prisons to a way
They come to build moral lives,
        And integrate to life's doorway.

Rejuvenate our inner cities.
        Give them work so they don't fail!
Educate where it is needed;
        Care for all; let love prevail.

Education is a socialist effort.
        All contribute to its zing.
Country's resources are of God.
        Give back to man so all can sing.

Total wealth of one per cent
        Is more than the lower ninety.
With politicians favoring people
        Money should spread aplenty.

Self interest turns a face?
        People riot if we fail!
So educate and improve
        The ways of life we hail.

Statistics from Newsweek Magazine,
February 23, 1998, p. 6.

FACTORY DOLLAR CHRONICLE

People buy goods the factories make.
        Workers make do with earnings they take.
But with no unions owners don't share
        What is needed for life to be fair.

'Well fixed' buy stocks to make a huge gain,
        On labor put forth in ardent pain.
Factories move for jobs on the cheap;
        Standards of living shift and we weep.

Our cities once made most everything used;
        But they are gutted and deficits fuse.
Politicians vie for business gold;
        Rewarding the corp's they get so bold.

Barriers come down so all compete;
        Worldwide goods fill our stores replete.
Automatics and cheap jobs come in;
        Humanity squirms for life to win.

People lose jobs and welfare runs out;
        The homeless are our country's curse.
Politicians turn their well fed faces.
        A Roosevelt Plan wouldn't be so terse.*

When automation swells with jobs too few,
        Will governments tax and spread revenue
So government jobs keep lives still proud;
        Or will the rich seek guard from the crowd?

*President Roosevelt put people to work through
starting government corporations.

HONORING GOD

We see on T.V. all wars are hell;
    Children and women they slaughter.
And men for 'honor' maim till fell;
    Ghastly becoming the Devil's fodder.

But God wades a different campaign -
    Where children and women we treasure.
God's 'Commands' form a singing refrain;
    His honor within making life a pleasure.

So through the U.N. get it backed
    That countries change its charter,
And aid any country that's attacked.
    So be it resolved with plans to occur.

With unions on behalf of workers,
    And mediation by governments,
Businesses will choose to share
    Money needed for worker intents.

Countries will not war each other,
    And money will flow for good of man;
So happiness reigns for all to grasp;
    With honoring God as man's great plan.

"Copyright permission Hammond Incorporated, Maplewood, N.J."

BOW WEST

With the Temple destroyed,
    And the West Wall remaining,
God's thoughts are now deployed;
    Bow West, God's Spirit's reclaiming.

God's Spirit's in the water;
    As in Genesis 'tis told.
There praise our kingly Father;
    Bow West as was foretold.

In James and Hudson Bays,
    Our Father asks for you.
Share eye of Communion with him
    For inner light to view.

EARTH'S JUDGMENT

Toward Hercules we spin in space;
    With God's Plan in us and earth.
Moving toward that constellation;
    Our judgment signed from birth.

Hercules speaks of Christ in space;
    Son of God and man on earth.
Earth's fate consigned to how we live
    God's Plan for us from birth.

Hercules carried a Devil's Club,
    And Christ commands God's show.
God gave those Ten for us to follow;
    His will through Christ to know.

Christ as Cygnus was overhead
    The night that I was born.
He's seen on Cross up in the sky.
    Christ's sign to help reform.

To right of cross is Lyra;
    Which Schiller named the Manger.*
Christ Child's head is Vega;
    Brightest star in the hemisphere.

Vega is a Spanish word.
    Moist meadow is what it means.
Christlike lives is what we need,
    For God to care for the greens.

Global warming spans the earth,
    And the Devil has his way.
People do whate'er they choose;
    Need turn to God to save the day.

* Schiller gave Christian names to the
  constellations.

Chart from Fieldbook of Natural History, by E. Laurence Palmer, 1949. Permission to reproduce from McGraw-Hill Book Company

I, DuWayne E. Oakes, was born at 3:00 A.M., May 28, 1926,
in Fillmore, Benson County, North Dakota.

Fillmore is in Benson County;
A county shaped like a shoe.
Ben carried God's Covenant for David.
God wanted it renewed.

North Dakota means Northern Ally;
God's Spirit in water tone.
Cygnus trumpets from sky on map.*
In North Dakota he is shown.

* Cygnus means Swan.

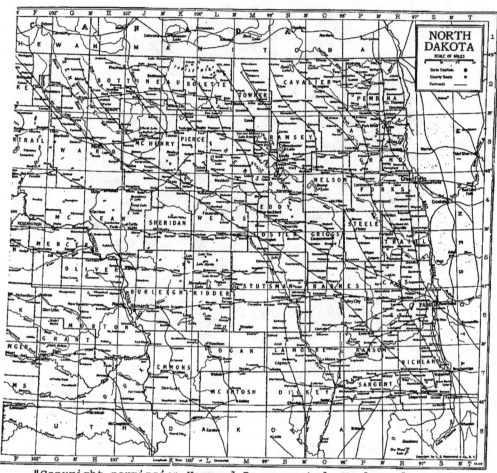

"Copyright permission Hammond Incorporated, Maplewood, N.J."

God planned Christ's Cross as Cygnus;
From Cross to map do thread.
Swan's head trumpeted at Minot*
Christ's call to me at Moorhead.*

* A Minot is a Paris measure of grain.
  A Moorhead is an African shaped head.

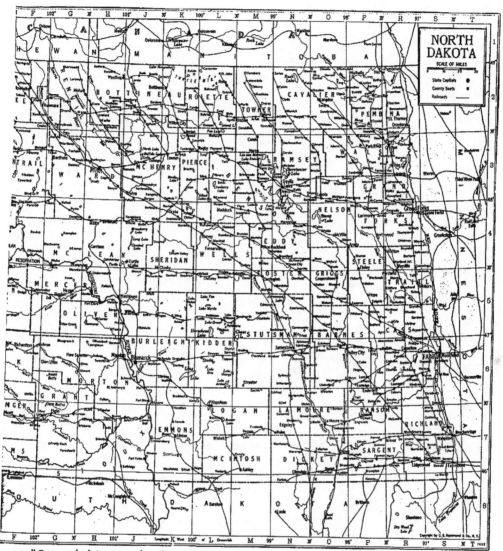

"Copyright permission Hammond Incorporated. Maplewood, N.J."

Christ's head is shown in Africa;
    Formed by God with horn on head.
Trumping head of Cygnus
    Hearkening to me at Moorhead.

It was in Moorhead, Minnesota,
    Where Christ beckoned to me as Light.
His inner Love consumed my soul,
    And showed me his steps so bright.

25

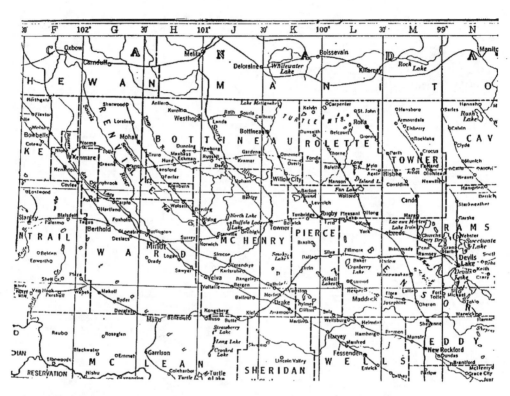

"Copyright permission Hammond Incorporated. Maplewood, N.J."

A PERSONAL ASSOCIATION

My Grandpa and Grandma Anderson
    Both worked on the railroads there
Where railroads form the womb
    Of our Patron Saint so fair.

Grandpa worked for the Great Northern;
    Both he and dad on the Soo Line.
After they moved to Fillmore,
    Grandma checked books in towns so fine.

26

JESUS TRUMPETS AS CYGNUS

Look at Jesus as the Swan;
    Its head's on map you see.
He trumpets at Minot, North Dakota;
    With Peter there, he does emcee.

Cygnus trumpets a Christmas Stocking;
    Renville County in wooden shape
Riding on Ward's wooden 'horse'.
    Like Jesus entered at stately gate.

Christ told Peter to found his church.
    To Rome he went and did it.
Now it's known throughout the world;
    Helping people be Godly fit.

Souris River forms a peter,
    And railroads form a vagina.
Colt with 'tail' of Gemini twins
    Christmas Stocking to the arena.

See twins that are formed in peter.
    In Egg and Sevenmile Creeks they tarry.
McHenry County's where there seen.
    Mack's a mild oath for Mary.

St. Mary is the Patron Saint
    Of the United States of America.
That oath because her womb you see
    In railroads of Dakota.

A Henry is an electrical charge;
    God used it for Christ's virgin birth.
It has been used to fertilize eggs.
    Mary's ovum felt God's worth.

See Fillmore in the narrowed womb.
    I was born there in the section house;
In nook just off the living room.
    Peter has twins it does espouse.

27

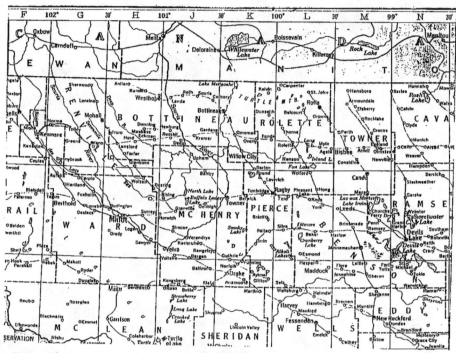

"Copyright permission Hammond Incorporated, Maplewood, N.J."

JESUS TRUMPETS HIS LIGHT

Renville means Rebirth Village.
    'Tis county shaped as a Christmas Stocking.
In it in Grano close to river
    Grandma's heart was caused to sing.

Italian word for grain is Grano;
    The grain for rebirth in Christ's Light.
Morris* appeared to Grandma
    After he'd drowned, 'twas God's foresight.

I was on the sofa sitting;
    To the upstairs Grandma had started.
There in the landing she saw him;
    She turned and told me his tread.

Town's people later told us
    A floodgate needed repair;
So Morris went with his father,
    Then drowned and appeared in the stair.

*After over forty years, I first called Morris Billy, his
brother I played with. Morris means Dark complexioned one.

GOD'S SPIRIT AND ME

A Spirit form like Ireland shaped,
        From sleep I awakened and wrestled.
My body engulfed in the Spirit;
        Like Jacob at Peniel we struggled.

My body writhed and moved about.
        Its meaning I could not atone.
Then out it went to our Christ Trees;
        Where the Star of David had shown.

Later I woke from sleep again;
        As my face was breathed upon.
Like Jesus breathed on his disciples;
        Infusing God's Spirit thereon.

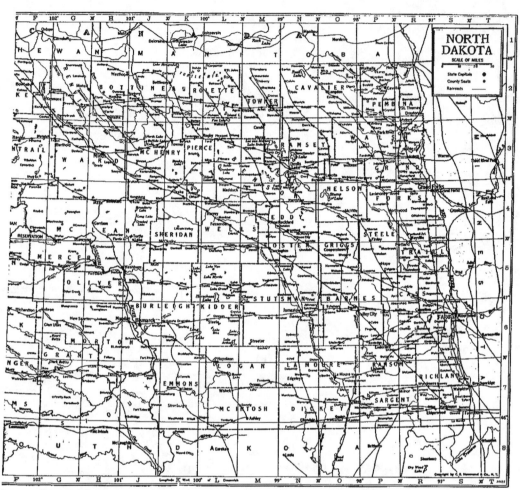

"Copyright permission Hammond Incorporated, Maplewood, N.J."

MELODY

Emmons, Logan and McIntosh Counties
    Are places you should look.
Formed in Beaver Creek and Railroad
    You'll find head of calf to man outlook.

Beneath the calf in South Dakota
    Dog's head is shaped in Missouri River;
Hearkens to David as the Dog Star.
    Map was new when Christ's Light did lure.

30

CYGNUS TRUMPETS MELODY

Melody's heralded as a sign
    That the Messiah's time is near.
First red heifer born in Israel
    Since the Temple was torn in fear.

A red heifer's ashes in water
    The priests of God they purified;
Before they entered his holy Temple,
    Where Arc of Covenant sanctified.

An 'arc' is a heavenly body's path.
    That path to map in the state
Where 'Cygnus' trumpets to Moorhead
    'Bout his African headed mate.

Find head of calf in south of map.
    Its head is formed with that of man
In Emmons and McIntosh Counties.
    Melody comes to 'speak' again.

Jesus called Peter the Rock
    On whom he would build his church.
A Peter's to north, two heads therein.
    My Gemini twin so search.

See head of dog in south of map.
    He shouts Eureka 'cause of calf.
Man's dam came and changed his form,
    But you can see God's river's path.

Long Lake is where God's seal is formed;
    In Burleigh and Kidder Counties.
Seals were used to make impressions;
    Like Melody to man foresees.

Jesus said he'd send another;
    A paraclete for believers pure.
Born in Fillmore, North Dakota,
    I wrote God's signs to reinsure.

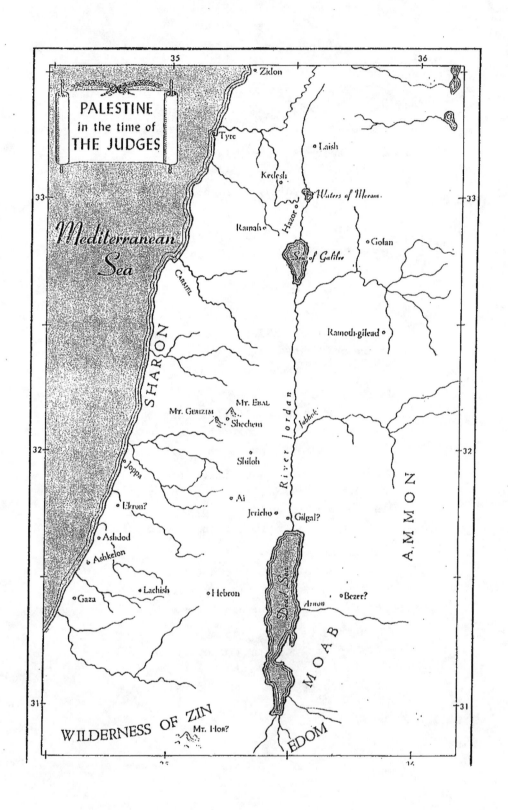

PALESTINE
in the time of
THE JUDGES

Mediterranean
Sea

° Zidon

Tyre

° Laish

Kedesh

Waters of Merom

Ramah °

Hazor

Golan °

Sea of Galilee

Ramoth-gilead °

CARMEL

S
H
A
R
O
N

Mт. Ebal

Mт. Gerizim

Shechem

River Jordan

Jabbok

Shiloh

A
M
M
O
N

Joppa

° Ai

Jericho ° ° Gilgal?

Ekron? °

° Ashdod

Dead Sea

° Ashkelon

° Lachish

° Hebron

Arnon

° Bezer?

° Gaza

M
O
A
B

WILDERNESS OF ZIN

Mт. Hor?

EDOM

DAVID AS CHRISTIAN

Sirius is called the Dog Star;
    Brightest star up in the sky.
Shiller renamed it David;
    Biblically he's there to vie.

Canis Major and Canis Minor;
    Two Dog stars up in the sky.
Canis Major is the brightest;
    As David it shines on high.

These dogs in earth were formed.
    The Dead Sea and Estonia framed them.
Estonia's shy with fertile head.
    The Dead Sea's changed, God's stratagem.

David came to mean Beloved.
    Tallinn is the Dog Star's eye.
God's love for Lord is not denied;
    David as Christian shines on high.

* The map of Estonia is on page ten.

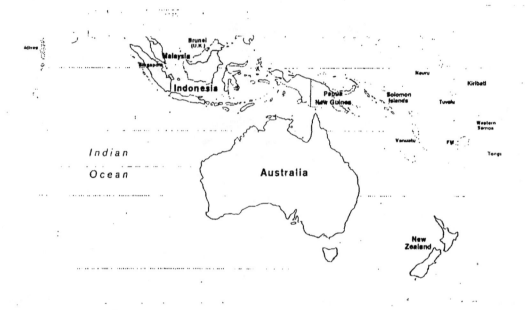

* The hammer-like indentation in top of Australia is Carpentaria
Gulf.

```
          GOD 'TRAILS YA'

Australia has our fetus' look;
     Its mouth is opened wide.
To have Communion with our God
     Was meant for Godly pride.

Canberra is the capital
     Built as eye of that land.
Meeting Place is what it means.
     For Christian growth it does stand.

Tasmania as a bread 'twas formed,
     Before we opened eyes.
And earthly Devils attacked that food;
     To sham what in us tries.

New Guinea as New Gold was claimed.*
     Carpenteria Gulf is near.
God placed it so you hear the screams
     When fetuses cry that God may hear.

God's gold was meant for all to share;
     With lives of pure concern.
Governments need a social care;
     With church advice for all to learn.

Judas, prominent in his land,
     As a hammer blow he came
When name was changed to Maccabee;
     For in that name it is the same.

Australia has a hammer dent;
     In Carpentaria Gulf 'tis formed.
'Twas as a carpenter Christ was bent;
     Before he preached and warned.

The head of Africa has like dent;
     To show the world its shame.
Christ's Communion too soon spent;
     Because of gold in Judas' name.

Other Judases now claim gold;
     Not meting out for good.
Politicians help them keep their hoards;
     Funds they need misunderstood.

Christ's head was formed in Africa;
     With Madagascar as the bread.
His tears are shown beneath the eye
     His foot's for you to tread.



* A guinea is an English gold coin.
```

'ANGEL LAND'

God's Spirit as angelic Ireland
    Flew to England as God's will.
Northern half of England's shape
    A bonneted lady it did fill.

It affected roots within my genes
    From Lady Hatfield to 'Grandpa' Oakes.
Such hatted ladies in her time
    Lived prime lives as noble folks.

England's shape in southern half
    Like that of sheep being shorn;
Sitting upright on its haunches,
    As some shearers plunk their form.

England has a special meaning,
    Coming from the Angli people;
Who from Denmark's Angel District*
    Went to England, were so thankful.

Peter's seen with keys in Denmark;
    Keys that open way to Godland.
Engli(e) people known as Engles
    Came from Peter's Angel Land.

Greenwich, England, is the place
    From which earth's time is figured.
God's Spirit helps with God's own plan.
    Time is granted if God's prefered.

God's Spirit in Ireland's form
    Goes to 'Angel Land' as England;
To do God's will throughout the earth;
    Helping people with God's stand.

* According to England's King Alred and
the chronicler Aethelweard   Engle means angel.

36

Isle of
Man

My Great Grandpa, James Hatfield Oakes, was named Hatfield to
carry on the family name of his mother who was a Hatfield.

INTERNAL CLEANSING

Baptism is a holy rite,
      God's love it does impart.
Through Father, Son and Spirit,
      He sends his love to heart.

In James and Hudson Bays
      God shows his form to us.
Through water with his word
      His being cleanses us.

That word the Ten Commandments;
      God gave them to obey.
His water does confirm it;
      Life's better then that way.

Confess your sins to God;
      Repent of evil ways.
Regenerate yourself
      And live for better days.

Wash feet for walk with Christ;
      A sign that you'll obey
The Ten Commandments given,
      That God may have a say.

"Copyright permission Hammond Incorporated, Maplewood, N.J."

GOD'S SPIRIT GOES RIGHT

God, Christ and Holy Spirit
    All in left have stand.
But, God's Plan has Ten Commands;
    As Spirit goes right to Holy Land.

It's how you feel in your heart
    That's your stand on each Command;
So God is master of your life;
    And all faiths see Holy Land.

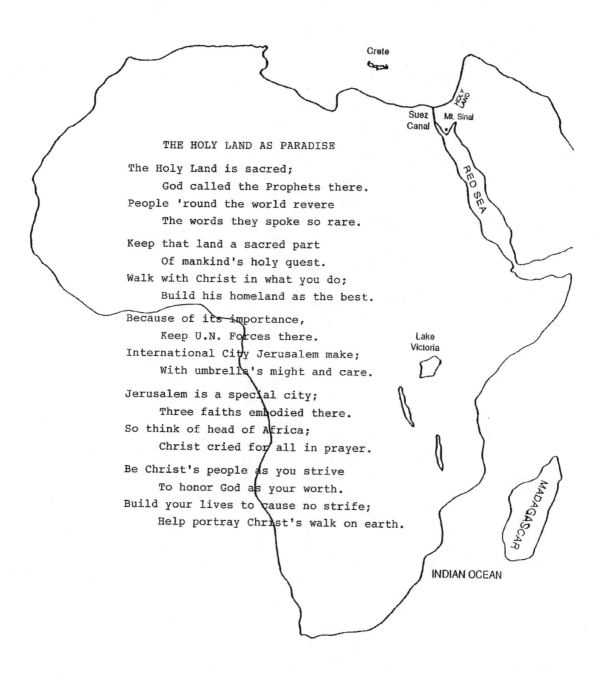

THE HOLY LAND AS PARADISE

The Holy Land is sacred;
    God called the Prophets there.
People 'round the world revere
    The words they spoke so rare.

Keep that land a sacred part
    Of mankind's holy quest.
Walk with Christ in what you do;
    Build his homeland as the best.

Because of its importance,
    Keep U.N. Forces there.
International City Jerusalem make;
    With umbrella's might and care.

Jerusalem is a special city;
    Three faiths embodied there.
So think of head of Africa;
    Christ cried for all in prayer.

Be Christ's people as you strive
    To honor God as your worth.
Build your lives to cause no strife;
    Help portray Christ's walk on earth.

Crete

Suez
Canal

HOLY
LAND

Mt. Sinai

RED SEA

Lake
Victoria

MADAGASCAR

INDIAN OCEAN

STAR DUST IN GOD'S LIGHT

God made us from our star.
    Star dust and water we are -
Developed by God's Light
    With elements from afar.

As food machines he made us;
    So energy in us flows
For thought and movement 'bout him;
    As Christ within us grows.

The Bible says God is Light;
    As Light Christ beckoned me.
Energy from him excited
    What he had made so free.

His Light controlled my being
    From tree that did not burn.
God sent his love to me;
    For it I'll always yearn.

God's Light from sun apart,
    Counter to magnetic force,
As in Ireland shown it came.
    God's Light was its own source.

God's special 'Light' fulfills
    His plan to our invite.
To herald his cause God formed us -
    Star dust, water and Light.

GOD'S LIGHT IS PARAMOUNT

God's Light summoned me from a Christ Tree and caused me to reveal his signs. It started at Christ's birth, as told by Joseph to James.

"Then I saw a woman coming down from the hill country, and she asked, 'Where are you going sir?'

"I replied, 'I am looking for a Hebrew midwife.'

"She inquired, 'Are you an Israelite?'

"I told her, 'Yes.'

"And she said, ' And who's the one having a baby in the cave?'

"I replied, 'My fiancee.'

"And she continued, 'She isn't your wife?'

"I said to her, 'She is Mary, who was raised in the temple of the Lord; I obtained her by lot as my wife. But she's not really my wife; she's pregnant by the holy spirit.'

"The midwife said, 'Really?'"

Joseph responded, "Come and see."

And the midwife went with him. As they stood in front of the cave, a dark cloud overshadowed it. The midwife said, "I've really been privileged, because today my eyes have seen a miracle in that salvation has come to Israel."

Suddenly the cloud withdrew from the cave and an intense light appeared inside the cave, so that their eyes could not bear to look. And a little later that light receded until an infant became visible; he took the breast of his mother Mary.

Then the midwife shouted: "What great day this is for me because I've seen this new miracle!"

The Apocryphon of The Infancy by James 19:1-17. The Complete Gospels.

43

Christ's Light beckoned and enticed me to write. Now, as an old man, some people are recognizing how God has worked through me. The following was written by John of the New Testament:

It happened one day when John, the brother of James - who are the sons of Zebedee - had come up to the temple, that a Pharisee named Arimanius approached him and said to him, "Where is your master whom you followed?" And he said to him, "He has gone to the place from which he came." The Pharisee said to him, "With deception did this Nazarine deceive you, and filled your ears with lies, and closed your hearts and turned you from the traditions of your fathers."

When I, John, heard these things I turned away from the temple to a desert place. And I grieved greatly in my heart saying, "How then was the savior appointed, and why was he sent into the world by his Father, and who is his Father who sent him, and of what sort is that aeon to which we shall go?

Straightway, while I was contemplating these things, behold the heavens opened and the whole creation which is below saw in the light a youth who stood by me. While I looked at him he became like an old man. And he changed his likeness again becoming like a servant. There was not a plurality before me, but there was a likeness with multiple forms in the light, and the likenesses appeared through each other, and the likenesses had three forms.

He said to me, "John, John, why do you doubt, or why are you afraid? You are not unfamiliar with the image are you? - that is, do not be timid! - I am the one who is with you always. I am the Father, I am the Mother, I am the Son. I am the undefiled and incorruptible one.

Now I have come to teach you what is and what was and what will come to pass, that you may know the things which are not revealed and those which are revealed, and to teach you concerning the unwavering race of the perfect Man. Now, therefore, lift up your face, that you may receive the things that I shall teach you today, and may tell them to your fellow spirits who are from the unwavering race of the perfect Man.

The Apocryphon of John 1:4-25, 30-32, 2:1-25 (second century) Nag Hammadi Library, Third Edition, pages 105-106.

GOD'S PLAN TO UNIFY

Jesus is this old man;
    In that he guided me.
His love controlled my being;
    Light signed from in his tree.

He caused me to expound,
    'God made the earth with plan.'
Christ called me as his paraclete;
    To tell this to all man.

Think of all world's people
    Claiming gods so differently.
God wants them brought together;
    His signs for unity.

So spread this word for God!
    He wants all people to obey
His plan of how to live;
    To join in his walkway.

After death your soul's controlled.
    God will say where it goes.
Do not limit realms of God.
    He recycles souls he knows.

God's Spirit comes to Isle of Man
    To Angel Land it flows.
After our resurrection
    We're like angels, God's repo's.*

Angels go to England.
    Lady and Lamb signed there.
Our spirits flow to Angel Land;
    England a Godland declare.

* We'll be like angels. (Luke 20:36)

45

CHRIST'S CALL TO ME

Then said Jesus to them again, Peace be unto
you: as my Father hath sent me, even so I
send you.
And when he had said this, he breathed on
them, and saith unto them, Receive ye the
Holy Ghost:

John 20:21-22

First Wednesday night of 74,
    I was awakened from sleep surprised,
Shook by a Spirit in Ireland's shape.
    'Twas like polarized Light comprised.

Awakened next week I lay there,
    And from right to left on my face
A breath of warm air I felt;
    As Christ's Spirit breathed his grace.

The following week I stirred again,
    And a voice like a charge resounded,
'You are my warden!" A keeper.
    Christ's Godhead call compounded.

God's call is shown in James and Hudson Bays;
    Sharing Communion on our continent;
That I may tell his earthly signs,
    And be for Christ a complement.

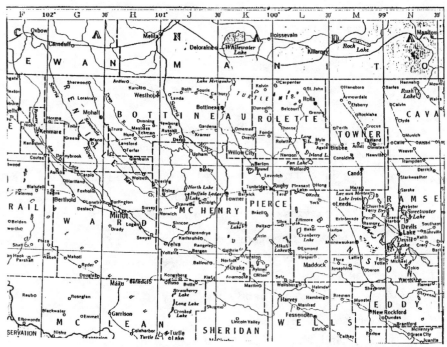

"Copyright permission Hammond Incorporated, Maplewood, N.J."

BORN OF OUR PATRON SAINT

A minister, while talking 'bout me,
    Said mine is the African head.
My head's the one that wrote God's Plan;
    So all people look and are fed.

Everyone has that God planned head;
    Made by him with his vested Plan.
I wrote 'bout signs God formed in it;
    So lives are lived in Godly span.

Born in the womb of our Patron Saint;*
    In Fillmore a Christmas Stocking
Shown for you on Ward County's Colt;
    Filled with signs God made to cling.

* St. Mary is the Patron Saint of the United States.
Her womb's on 100° Meridian West in North Dakota.

47

THE SOUL'S DIMENSION

Kathy's spirit left her body,
    When her car rolled down a hill.
From out of her car - up above
    She viewed the scene, 'twas God's will.

In shock! She thought of her family,
    And prayed to God on high:
"Dear God, don't take me now!
    My family needs me I cry."

Her soul went back into her body,
    And she lives for us to know
God has another dimension;
    Where good souls are sure to go.

God shows his Spirit in Ireland
    Coming to this Isle of Man.
Help your soul seek God's Spirit;
    Walk with Christ to make that span.

God's Spirit lives as life eternal;
    Traveling to our distant shore;
Guiding souls to join with him;
    That they live forevermore.

SPREAD GOD'S LOVE

Because we have a God of love,
    He imbued that love in us.
And parents love their children;
    With loving care a Godly plus.

When we extend God's loving care,
    To friends and in the workplace,
God's kind care they come to know;
    And lives are bettered in his grace.

The Devil thrives on gnashing teeth,
    And wars that kill God's people.
Stop the Devil and his strife;
    With Ten Commandments lived to full.

PROGRAM FOR GOD

By the way that we live,
      And exposure in our lives,
We're programmed to be good;
      Or for the Devil's cruel drives.

Jesus told us to be good,
      And kind to others too,
To build in us God's spirit
      So Commandments follow through.

When children play to kill
      They're learning sinful drives.
Keep them from such things;
      So God in them survives.

Good examples they do need
      In wholesome family life.
Think together with your spouse;
      So children start no strife.

When we're kind to others,
      We fill their hearts with love;
And build their hearts engrained
      With Commandments from above.

God is love the Bible says;
      As Christians help it spread.
Strive for loving ways to do;
      So better world is tread.

When Devil's route is trod,
      Dreadful things you come to pay.
So walk in love of Christ;
      Take his hand on life's highway.

IDENTIFICATION

Go to church and learn 'bout God;
    Attend the lessons too.
Fellowship with Christian friends;
    Live the life God wants for you.

Don't neglect your God in life,
    Put him in the things you do.
Live with Christ hand in hand;
    Ask his help to see you through.

After dinner read the Bible;
    With timely verses right for you.
Family life will come to flourish,
    As you learn God's point of view.

Be sure to speak your best for him;
    So others want to listen.
Make your life a Godly theme;
    For Christlike life to hasten.

Best think and do all that you need
    To live God's wholesome creed.
Look your best and say and do
    God's Plan through Christ for you.

BRAINS THAT CHANGE

Father loves son and mother her daughter.
> This relationship we proudly foster.
But done to excess our brains we inspire;
> So same sex connections we come to desire.

When mother tends to pamper her son
> So as a daughter his fortune is won,
And father tomboys his daughter's fem,
> Our children are nurtured obliquely then.

A 'homo' brain is different we think;
> It physically grows an aberrant kink.
What about children funly cavorting;
> Do same sex 'friends' have brains that go sporting?

Are genetic changes chemically formed;
> Spurred by emotions and wily porned?
Then life as we know it will tend to change;
> If it becomes mod to be homo and range.

Will hermaphrodites increase or be few,
> If neutering sex is the thing to do?
Best not take chances with lives to come;
> Be straight in your life and pride what is done.

We read in Leviticus 18:22
> Homosexuality is hated by God.
Yet, there are those who tempt God's wrath;
> Christ's way is askewed in their path.

We've seen the pup that suckles the cat,
> And brood chicken's ducklings loved and fat.
You know your instincts can go askew;
> So guide and control the things that you do.

PROTECT OUR EARTH

Africa was overgrazed,
    So desert land was formed.
Now holes get big in ozone layer,
    Melting glaciers we are warned.

Warming oceans change their currents;
    Worsened storms they do provoke.
So stop polluting earth's pure air
    With auto smog and factory smoke.

Regenerate the ozone layer;
    Slow the glaciers' melting.
Quickly turn to smogless autos;
    Stop world's factories from polluting.

Keep world's forests at high level;
    Stop the burning of the trees.
Atmosphere and land are changing;
    Slow the 'storms' with expertise.

SAVE OUR EARTH

Stars endure cyclic changes;
      As do planets in their throes.
But, see the Devil's work in Mars;
      His way of life stops all that grows.

Here on Earth we have Christ's message
      'Bout God's Plan and way to last.
The counties at the end of horn
      Speak to us as names do cast.

County means Domain of Lord,
      And state the nature of the counties.
So think of meanings as you look;
      Then God's Plan will come with ease.

County Cass means Cash and Case,
      And Ransom means Deliver From Sin.
Christ's Case to Ransom County Richland
      Cloudy Water so life we win.

Christ trumps Case for Minnesota;
      Cloudy Water is its meaning.
Derived from Souix for God's teach in.
      But, Devil life stops God's cling.

Christ trumps to us Free From Sin
      The Richland God has made for us.
Spread God's Plan to all the people!
      Make his life a worthy plus.

Use Cash to close the ozone holes.
      Scientists say what needs be done.
Rise up in action to their call,
      And do God's will so life is won.

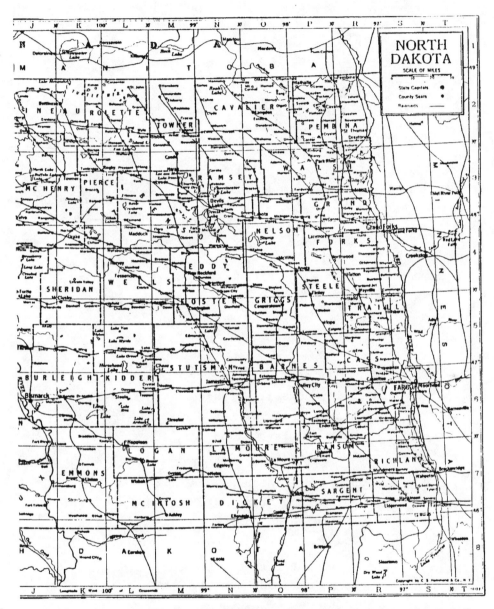

"Copyright permission Hammond Incorporated. Maplewood, N.J."

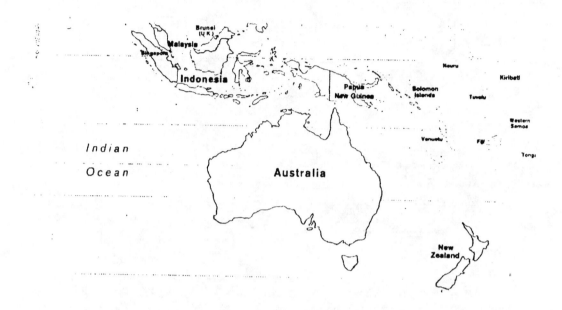

FETUS MESSAGE

Australia shows its message;
    Shaped as a fetus aspiring.
Communion cup it strives for.
    God given life so desiring.

New Guinea o'er head as New Gold
    With Judas grasping for means.
So fetus child he hammers
    God's Law of life to smithereens.

Thou shall not kill God told us,
    Earth's masses humanly control.
Pollutants caused by too many
    Destroy the environs resole.

MAD A GAS CAR

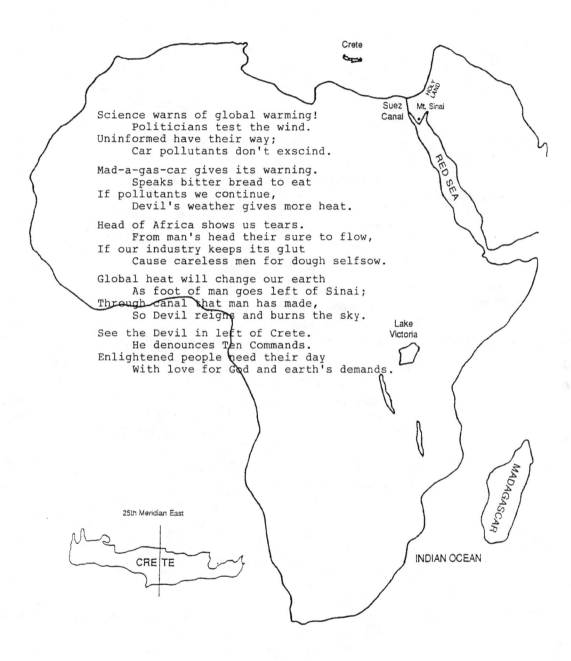

Science warns of global warming!
    Politicians test the wind.
Uninformed have their way;
    Car pollutants don't exscind.

Mad-a-gas-car gives its warning.
    Speaks bitter bread to eat
If pollutants we continue,
    Devil's weather gives more heat.

Head of Africa shows us tears.
    From man's head their sure to flow,
If our industry keeps its glut
    Cause careless men for dough selfsow.

Global heat will change our earth
    As foot of man goes left of Sinai;
Through canal that man has made,
    So Devil reigns and burns the sky.

See the Devil in left of Crete.
    He denounces Ten Commands.
Enlightened people need their day
    With love for God and earth's demands.

FOLLOW CHRIST

Hearken to the call of God!
    Do those things he wants you to.
He made signs for you to know
    Life with him he wants for you.

Leaders lead with Ten Commandments;
    Help God's people banish sin.
Walk with Christ in what you do;
    Help all people walk with him.

When countries go to war and fight
    It's sinful how they kill!
Build on treaties we now have;
    Rights with love we need fulfill.

Don't hearken to the Devil's ways;
    God's loving care will end.
Don't let your soul burn in hell!
    On Christ you must depend.

Reflect Christ's word in your life;
    Repent of sin and evil ways.
Be baptized in God's own water;
    Let Christ's kindness lead your days.

Make it easy for God's people;
    U.N. Rights you need to champion.
Right the wrongs of selfish thinking;
    Better life with what is done.

UNIVERSAL DECLARATION OF HUMAN RIGHTS

BY THE GENERAL ASSEMBLY OF THE UNITED NATIONS

1948

PREAMBLE

Whereas recognition of the inherent dignity and of the equal and inalienable rights of all members of the human family is the foundation of freedom, justice and peace in the world, and

Whereas disregard and contempt for human rights have resulted in barbarous acts which have outraged the conscience of mankind, and the advent of a world in which human beings shall enjoy freedom of speech and belief and freedom from fear and want has been proclaimed as the highest aspiration of the common people, and

Whereas it is essential, if man is not to be compelled to have recourse, as a last resort, to rebellion against tyranny and oppression that human rights should be protected by the rule of law, and

Whereas it is essential to promote the development of friendly relations between nations, and

Whereas the peoples of the United Nations have in Charter reaffirmed their faith in fundamental human rights, in the dignity and worth of the human person and in the equal rights of men and women, and determined to promote social progress and better standards of life in larger freedom, and

Whereas the Member States have pledged themselves to achieve, in co-operation with the United Nations, the promotion of universal respect for and the observance of human rights and fundamental freedoms, and

Whereas a common understanding of these rights and freedoms is of the greatest importance for the full realization of this pledge,

Now therefore,

THE GENERAL ASSEMBLY

PROCLAIMS this Declaration of Human Rights as a common standard of achievement for all peoples and all nations, to the end that every individual and every organ of society, keeping this declaration constantly in mind, shall strive by teaching and education to promote respect for these rights and freedoms and by progressive measures, national and international, to secure their universal and effective recognition and observance, both among the peoples of member states themselves and among the peoples territories under their jurisdiction.

ARTICLE 1. All human beings are born free and equal, in dignity and rights. They are endowed with reason and conscience, and should act towards one another in spirit of brotherhood.

ARTICLE 2. Everyone is entitled to all the rights and freedoms set forth in this declaration, without distinction of any kind, such as race, color, sex, language, religion, political or other opinion, national or social origin, property, birth or status.

Furthermore, no distinction shall be made on the basis of the political, jurisdictional or international status of the country or territory to which a person belongs, whether it be independent, Trust, Nonself-Governing or under any other limitation of sovereignty.

ARTICLE 3. Everyone has the right to life, liberty and security of person.

ARTICLE 4. No one shall be held in slavery or servitude; slavery and slave trade shall be prohibited in all their forms.

ARTICLE 5. No one shall be subjected to torture or to cruel, inhuman or degrading treatment or punishment.

ARTICLE 6. Everyone has the right to recognition everywhere as a person before the law.

ARTICLE 7. All are equal before the law and are entitled without discrimination to equal protection of the law. All are entitled to equal protection against any discrimination in violation of this Declaration and against any incitement to such discrimination.

ARTICLE 8. Everyone has the right to an effective remedy by competent national tribunals for acts violating the fundamental rights granted him by the Constitution or by law.

ARTICLE 9. No one shall be subjected to arbitrary arrest, detention or exile.

ARTICLE 10. Everyone is entitled in full equality to fair and public hearing by an independent and impartial tribunal, in the determination of his rights and obligations and of any criminal charge against him.

ARTICLE 11. 1. Everyone with a penal offense has the right to be presumed innocent until proved guilty according to law in a public trial at which he has all the guarantees necessary for his defense.

2. No one shall be held guilty on any penal offense on account of any act or omission which did not constitute a penal offense, under national or international law, at the time when it was committed. Nor shall a heavier penalty be imposed than the one that was applicable at the time the penal offense was committed.

ARTICLE 12. No one shall be subjected to arbitrary interference with his privacy, family home or correspondence, nor to attacks upon his honor and reputation. Everyone has the right to the protection of the law against such interference or attacks.

ARTICLE 13. 1. Everyone has the right to freedom of movement and residence within the borders of each state.

2. Everyone has the right to leave any country, including his own, and to return to his country.

ARTICLE 14. 1. Everyone has the right to seek and to enjoy in other countries asylum from persecution.

2. This right may not be invoked in the case of prosecutions genuinely arising from nonpolitical crimes or from acts contrary to the purposes and principles of the United Nations.

ARTICLE 15. 1. Everyone has the right to nationality.

2. No one shall be arbitrarily deprived of his nationality nor denied the right to change his nationality.

ARTICLE 16. 1. Men and women of full age, without any limitation due to race, nationality or religion, have the right to marry and to found a family. They are entitled to equal rights as to marriage, during marriage and at its dissolution.

2. Marriage shall be entered into only with free and full consent of the intending spouses.

3. The family is the natural and fundamental group unit of society and is entitled to protection by society and the State.

ARTICLE 17. 1. Everyone has the right to own property alone as well as in association with others.

2. No one shall be arbitrarily deprived of his property.

ARTICLE 18. Everyone has the right to freedom of thought, conscience and religion; this right includes freedom to change his religion or belief, and freedom, either alone or in community with others and in public or private, to manifest his religion or belief, and freedom, either alone or in community with others and in public or private, to manifest his religion or belief in teaching, practice, worship and observance.

ARTICLE 19. Everyone has the right to freedom of opinion and expression; this right includes freedom to hold opinions without interference and to seek, receive and impart information and ideas through any media and regardless of frontiers.

ARTICLE 20. 1. Everyone has the right to freedom of peaceful assembly and association.

2. No one may be compelled to belong to an association.

ARTICLE 21. 1. Everyone has the right to take part in the Government of his country, directly or through freely chosen representatives.

2. Everyone has the right of equal access to public service in his country.

3. The will of the people shall be the basis of the authority of government; this will shall be expressed in periodic and genuine elections which shall be by universal and equal suffrage and shall be held by secret vote or by equivalent free voting procedures.

ARTICLE 22. Everyone, as a member of society, has the right to social security and is entitled to the realization, through national effort and international co-operation and in accordance with the organization and resources of each state, of the economic, social and cultural rights indispensable for his dignity and free development of his personality.

ARTICLE 23. 1. Everyone has the right to work, to free choice of employment, to just and favorable conditions of work and to protection against unemployment.

2. Everyone, without discrimination, has the right to equal pay for equal work.

3. Everyone who works has the right to just and favorable remuneration insuring for himself and his family an existence worthy of human dignity, and supplemented, if necessary, by other means of social protection.

4. Everyone has the right to form and to join trade unions for the protection of his interests.

ARTICLE 24. Everyone has the right to rest and leisure, including reasonable limitation of working hours and periodic holidays with pay.

ARTICLE 25. 1. Everyone has the right to a standard of living adequate for the health and well-being of himself and his family, including food, clothing, housing and medical care and necessary social services, and the right to security in the event of unemployment, sickness, disability, widowhood, old age or other lack of livelihood in circumstances beyond his control.

2. Motherhood and childhood are entitled to special care and assistance. All children, whether born in or out of wedlock, shall enjoy the same social protection.

ARTICLE 26. 1. Everyone has the right to education. Education shall be free, at least in the elementary and fundamental stages. Elementary education shall be made generally available, and higher education shall be equally accessible to all on the basis of merit.

2. Education shall be directed to the full development of the human personality and to the strengthening of respect for human rights and fundamental freedoms. It shall promote understanding, tolerance and friendship among all nations, racial or religious groups, and shall further the activities of the United Nations for the maintenance of peace.

3. Parents have a prior right to choose the kind of education that shall be given to their children.

ARTICLE 27. 1. Everyone has the right freely to participate in the cultural life of the community, to enjoy the arts and to share in scientific advancement and its benefits.

2. Everyone has the right to the protection of the moral and material interests resulting from any scientific, literary or artistic production of which he is the author.

ARTICLE 28. Everyone is entitled to a social and international order in which the rights and freedoms set forth in this declaration can be fully realized.

ARTICLE 29. 1. Everyone has duties to the community in which alone the free and full development of his personality is possible.

2. In the exercise of his rights and freedoms, everyone shall be subject only to such limitations as are determined by law solely for the purpose of securing due recognition and respect for the rights and freedoms of others and of meeting the just requirements of morality, public order and the general welfare in a democratic society.

3. These rights and freedoms may in no case be exercised contrary to the purposes and principles of the United Nations.

ARTICLE 30. Nothing in this declaration may be interpreted as implying for any state, group or person, any right to engage in any activity or to perform any act aimed at the destruction of any of the rights and freedoms set forth herein.

The Universal Declaration of Human Rights by the General Assembly of the United Nations represents God working through people for an improvement of rights through their governments.

Crete

HOLY LAND

Suez Canal   Mt. Sinai

RED SEA

If you work for God's earthly kingdom, "...they shall beat their swords into plowshares, and their spears into pruning hooks: nation shall not lift up sword against nation, neither shall they learn war any more." Isaiah 2:4. This is depicted in a statue which Russia gave to the United Nations. We all need to fight for God's peace and defeat the Devil's cohorts who want wars. The countries of the United Nations need to emphasize God's will for people as he formed it in the head of Africa. Countries need to wipe away from their constitutions all laws that impede the growth of Christianity. And, special consideration needs to be given the worship of God. He made those signs on earth because he does not want to be ignored. He gave us a dominant message on our earth. Recognize it, and give support to God caring peaceful lives for all people.

Change the United Nations so that no permanent member of the Security Council can veto the will of the majority of the General Assembly. This will no longer permit a veto by just one member on the Security Council to override the will of the majority. Cause the United Nations to evolve into the United States of the World; initially establishing a time without penalties for countries to incorporate the Universal Declaration of Human Rights in their constitutions, gradually unifying the rights of all people. The United Nations needs to secure the boundaries of member countries; through amending its Charter so all countries come to the aid of any country that is attacked. There will then be less need for individual countries to have militaries, and the United Nations should evolve into having the world's only peace keeping force. This will cause huge amounts of money and resources now going into the militaries for death and destruction to be spent for people needs.

Lake Victoria

Countries should work through the United Nations for a controlled biosphere; so the earth's population does not exceed its sustainable resources and food growth; creating worldwide famine, and continue polluting the environment. Be proud as you do your part to build the Kingdom of God on earth, "And when he was demanded of the Pharisees, when the kingdom of God should come, he answered them and said, the kingdom of God cometh not with observation: Neither shall they say, Lo here! or lo there! for, behold, the kingdom is within (or, in the midst of) you." Luke 17:20-21

MADAGASCAR

INDIAN OCEAN

Crete

HOLY LAND

Suez Canal   Mt. Sinai

RED SEA

Moses' extended legal code is similar to that of Hammurabi's, which still exists on an obelisk. Scholars believe it was common in the Middle East at that time. It is believed that Hammurabi accumulated his from the thinking and practices of many different people. The Universal Declaration of Human Rights by the General Assembly of the United Nations contains those rights agreed to in our time. This is evidence of God working through people in nations so we evolve into his image in deeds. To enhance this, leaders need to incorporate these Human Rights in their countries' constitutions, and strive to improve them both.

When God first formed man, he did not know what sin is. But, before God did it, he wanted all people to love one another and live in peace; so he showed the way to eternal life through creating people in the image of his son Jesus Christ, who he symbolized in the head of Africa. He then gave Moses the Ten Commandments at Mt. Sinai, so mankind would come to know what it is to sin. Later, he caused Jesus Christ to be born, and imbued his Holy Spirit in him. Jesus gave us the gift of Holy Communion in remembrance of him, and called himself the bread of life. God proved this through forming the head of Africa symbolic of that of Jesus, with Madagascar as his footshaped bread, walking in Communion with God. He also caused Jesus to tell Peter that he was the Rock on whom he was going to found his church. God wants everybody to know this, and expects leaders to be Christians. Because the Ten Commandments say, "You shall not kill," leaders are expected to not start wars. If they do, they condemn themselves and their followers to hell. God exemplified in the head of Africa the tears they will experience in eternity, if their feet take the wrong turn at Mt. Sinai. Jesus' foot-like Bread of Communion will lead you to Paradise. Through this earliest form of writing, a seal, God has shown that he has given all judgment to his Son. He wants all killing, by the state and otherwise, to stop. Jesus said, "Blessed are the peacemakers; for they shall be called the children of God." Matthew 5:9. It's awesome that we on earth, with God's inscription on it and us, are swirling toward the Constellation Hercules; the half god and half man, who was known as the Averter of Evil. We either evolve towards God's will, or the Devil will win and destroy the earth.

Lake Victoria

MADAGASCAR

INDIAN OCEAN

64

BEGINNING TO END

Sugar is in the clouds
    That form the heavens' stars;
Which whirl to form the planets;
    So God planned life is ours.

Glycoaldehyde combines
    With molecules that spawn
D.N.A. for all our lives;
    Through God's Spirit in the dawn.

Astrophysicists now know
    Intelligence sweeps through space;
Through pulsars as they speak,
    Their signals interlace.

They signal 'bout life's trackings;
    Hum God's Spirit throughout all space.
Send his Spirit to his 'earths';
    Helping God in his grace.

Ireland shows as God's Spirit
    Coming to this Isle of Man;
Doing work as God directs;
    Saving planet is his plan.

Africa cries with Jesus' judgment,
    As our heads resolve our plight.
On to Hercules our earth spins;
    Preset Plan as God's showsite.

Peter holds salvation's key
    For life in Spirit form.
On to Godland ours will go,
    If Communion foot's our norm.

Kathy's spirit was so real
    When she saw her body form.
Where ours goes is God's resolve;
    To be with God or Devil shorn.

CHRISTIAN LADY

Peloponesia with face of a lady
    Flees the Devil and prides her ways.
That Christian lady strives with God;
    Cultivates love for Christ in days.

She knows the Devil can entice,
    Ruin her life with sinful luring.
Best walk with Christ as she strives
    For Christian life that is enduring.

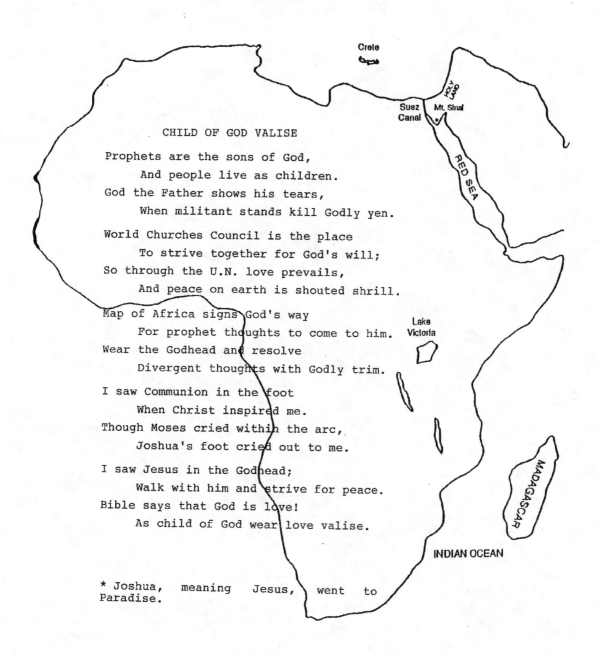

CHILD OF GOD VALISE

Prophets are the sons of God,
    And people live as children.
God the Father shows his tears,
    When militant stands kill Godly yen.

World Churches Council is the place
    To strive together for God's will;
So through the U.N. love prevails,
    And peace on earth is shouted shrill.

Map of Africa signs God's way
    For prophet thoughts to come to him.
Wear the Godhead and resolve
    Divergent thoughts with Godly trim.

I saw Communion in the foot
    When Christ inspired me.
Though Moses cried within the arc,
    Joshua's foot cried out to me.

I saw Jesus in the Godhead;
    Walk with him and strive for peace.
Bible says that God is love!
    As child of God wear love valise.

* Joshua, meaning Jesus, went to Paradise.

67

SPREAD GOD'S LOVE

God is Love so nourish him -
    In your life to God be true.
Don't restrict his love from others;
    Spread God's love in all you do.

Fill your life with kindness
    Doing good to all you can.
As God's children we are siblings;
    Helping him with his great plan.

Chart from Fieldbook of Natural History, by E. Laurence Palmer,
1949. Permission to reproduce from McGraw-Hill Book Company

GREAT DRAGON'S CLOSE TO CHRIST CHILD

In Tsingtao, China, I met a man
    Who talked with me about one God.
This stately man was kind and tempered,
    An intellectual with mind to prod.

In Tientsin I met another man
    Whose friendship I came to admire.
Mr. Chao was a wisened jeweler;
    From emperor line, he did inspire.

Together we journeyed to then 'Peiping';
    Where his ancestors once did rule;
To an outdoor religious court yard,
    Where Taoists gazed at stars to school.

See the Great Dragon on the chart;
    As Draco, the Dragon, he's known.
Plane of earth's orbit is in him;
    With Christian stars he is shown.

ONE GOD THROUGH CHRIST

Our governor was Gary Lock,
    Who champions a Chinese descent.
Grandfather was born in China,
    Where Gary and family went.

Ancient Chinese were Taoists;
    Believing in Tao, a cosmic force.
Its opposites of Yin and Yang
    Made heaven and earth in course.

They in turn made all creatures.
    Energy eternal formed man;
Who should live a selfless life
    To reach Tao in paradise plan.

That Cosmic Force is Christian God;
    His Spirit sent to 'Isle of Man'.
It's shown in Ireland's form on map.
    Spread this word to all you can.

Around the world in other places,
    Prophets aspired to God.
But God chose Christ for earthly plan,
    And Ten Commandments for to trod.

God beckons you with signs on earth;
    He made for all to see.
So hearken to his heavenly call;
    That you with him may be.

A CHRISTIAN SOCIALIST VIEW

The Declaration of Human Rights,
    By U.N. Member States,
Give religious rights to all;
    To choose their own dictates.

That's freedom to change religion;
    To practice, teach and observe;
Alone or with others,
    In public or private preserve.

Those Human Rights say to us
    Protect from loss of jobs.
So legislate and improve
    The life that in us throbs.

When people lose their jobs,
    So jobless rate is high,
Companies run by government
    Should open jobs to rectify.

Ninety per cent have less wealth
    Than upper one per cent.
Social taxes should produce
    A life with caring bent.

Our country has advanced
    As business it supports.
But God wants social conscience;
    For sharing Christian efforts.

Social countries should not war
    With private enterprise.
Use the best that both provide
    To help God's people's lives.

We're all God's children;
    As his signs for us do tell.
He cares for all to thrive;
    Helping others with the swell.

CHANNEL DRIVES FOR GOOD

People are more learned
    Than when grandpa went to school.
Evolvements now compete;
    New media makes us drool.

People see what they like
    From other countries now;
Learn of how to better lives,
    And some that's old comes to bow.

New ideas do surpass
    The thoughts of Marx's day.
Lower costs give more time
    To gain a schooled walkway.

Learned people want a say
    In what their countries do.
Issues studied for their merit
    Create new points of view.

Governments need to respond
    To people's learned thoughts.
Give them part in what is done.
    Propaganda's lost its days.

Help them vote for their man.
    Right to vote all clamor for.
Want make choices in their lives;
    Help the masses better soar.

Initiatives help the ways of man.
    Let the people start a cause.
Referendums fill a need.
    Help the people add their chaws.

Countries can incorporate
    These things in government.
Adds fulfillment to man's life;
    Helps rectify where not content.

BROTHER KEEPERS
COMMANDMENT KEEPERS

Newspaper, magazine & T.V. heads
    Flood reporters to their man;
Causing hype to tell the people
    Elect for President our showman.

People rally to their outcry;
    Money flows to their campaign.
Others struggle for some money;
    But campaigns go down the drain.

Politicians with most fleecing hands
    In pockets of the corporate heads
Insure that office will be theirs;
    Doing work as corporate feds.

Corporate fascism we do get
    When corporations say whose in.
Social conscience loses out
    As people's will takes a downspin.

Reform the financing for campaigns;
    Help our democracy last.
Let people say who are their reps;
    Keep social conscience in their grasp.

Poverty plagues one fourth of children;
    Think of lives their apt to spawn.
Taxing wealthy sure could build
    Gov. corporations as social dawn.

One third of working families
    Have no health insurance at all.
Yet in every modern country
    Socialized medicine cares for all.

Roosevelt plans were caring plans;
    Four terms they voted him in.
Gov. corporations we still do need -
    God's love for poor express for him.

BE CHRISTIAN FAIR

Life was different in grandpa's day.
    Most people farmed the land.
Farmers gave their hired hands
    Land to grow to make a stand.

Now through taxes that we pay,
    We help our people thrive.
Happy people we do have
    When life is fair to strive.

Schools are funded by the people.
    Colleges receive a share
Of social money so to bloom;
    So people prosper everywhere.

When our people give so much
    To help our children strive,
They must expect when they are grown
    To help our country thrive.

When one percent make same money
    As all of lower ninety,
One percent should pay one half
    Of taxes paid in federal fee.

What percent of country's money
    Do top percents of earners make?
Percents that make the most of it
    Need share the same in tax outtake.

When people pay the same percent
    Of earnings that they make,
Lower earners are most hurt,
    Cause taxes shrink their needs intake.

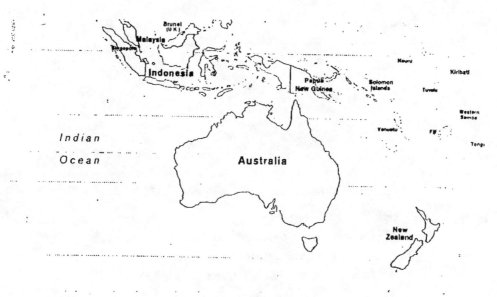

PARADISE OR GOLD

New Guinea means New Gold.
    'Tis shown upon the map.
It acts as the hammer
    Giving fetus such a tap
That Australia squirms for life,
    And Tasmanian Bread's no hap.
If New Gold kills the fetus,
    God's Communion it does scrap,
And leg to right of Sinai
    As New Zealand it does snap;
So Paradise is lost,
    If love is not the map.
God is love the Bible says.
    Show his love in country's track.
Help the church give to others.
    Make country's love a Godly pact.
Solomon's the wise man;
    Christian brothers show your tact.

* Papua New Guinea is part of the island of New Guinea.

RESURRECT THROUGH CHRIST

Jesus Christ was crucified
    Cause his thoughts roiled the state.
Yet today his thoughts live on.
    His love for man touched our fate.

God calls you to feed and heal;
    With Christ's love inside your head.
Cause of life to think like Christ;
    So his love is never dead.

Look at Christ as the cause
    To think your nature through.
Resurrect your goals in life;
    Christ in mind as you renew.

MARY MOTHER OF LIFE

Christ as love imbued my soul
  So Communion did enthrall me.
Then when Grandma's form I saw
  His love again came out for thee.

Christ trumpets signs he came to show
  In state where I was born.
North Dakota means Northern Allie;
  Look to North to see Eve's form.

Adam means Earth and Eve means Life;
  Water of 'Life' you've come to see.
In North Dakota you've seen the womb
  Of Northern Allie with life giving key.

Pope Pius IX proclaimed
  Christ's Mother Mary, Mother of God,
As Patron Saint of the United States.*
  Christ trumpets sights for you to 'trod'.

* Pope Pius IX confirmed doctrine
declaring Mary, Mother of Jesus
Christ, as Patron Saint of the United
States.

ANGELIC DOVES

Kathy's spirit went out of body,
    And she viewed it from above.
She lived a stint in spirit life;
    Akin to God sent Angel Dove.

It may be said magnetic force
    Kathy's soul had entered in.
When she viewed herself so grim,
    God's own force she entered in.

Stars with planets are in motion.
    God looks down at what he's done
From dimension that's all knowing;
    Sending Spirits when time's come.

The Bible says we'll be like angels;
    Shown by God in Ireland's shape.
Clue to us of distant journey;
    To other 'Isles' of God's landscape.

Our earth spins on to Hercules;
    Son of Zeus the Olympic god.
Olympia, capital of my state,
    With Olympic Mountains I have trod.

God looks down from Hudson Bay;
    At my state of Washington.
God signed state of cleansing water;
    Through walk with Christ then angel on.

Christ in Africa speaks like James;
    Ten Commandments for to follow.
Hercules works for Christian God
    Viewing worlds in his tableau.

GOD HERALDS
TO WASHINGTOWN

Greeks called Hercules son of Zeus;
    The one who fathered Olympic 'gods'.
Olympic gods like 'gods' of worlds;
    Ruled by Zeus with his prods.

Olympic Mountains I oft see
    In Washington; my present state.
Olympia kin to capital
    From which space signals generate.

Jupiter was the Roman Zeus.
    Saturn was the 'sower god'.
They aligned as Bethlehem Star,*
    When Christ was born with promenade.

Christian God like Zeus looks down
    From James and Hudson Bays.
His 'Washingtown' is Washington;
    To set the stage for God's days.

* When Jupiter and Saturn converged the summer of 1981, Karlis Kaufmanis, a Lutheran astronomer, was notarized for saying it happened as the Star of Bethlehem.

Ton is the suffix for town.

GOD'S PLAN PROVES JESUS
Through Land And Water Formations

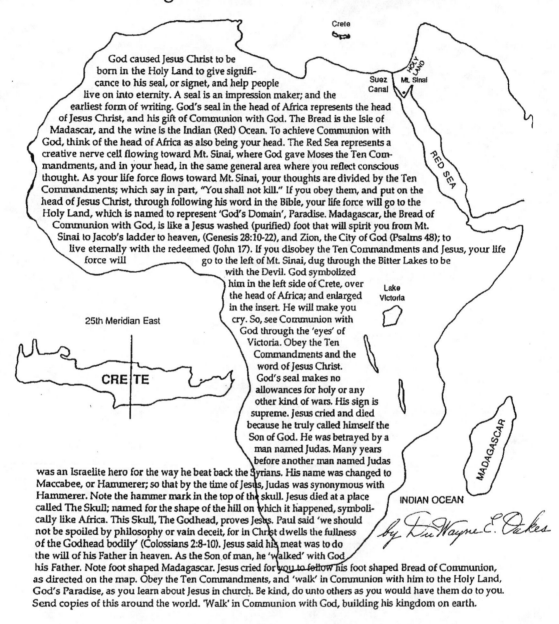

Crete

Holy Land

Suez Canal

Mt. Sinai

RED SEA

God caused Jesus Christ to be born in the Holy Land to give significance to his seal, or signet, and help people live on into eternity. A seal is an impression maker; and the earliest form of writing. God's seal in the head of Africa represents the head of Jesus Christ, and his gift of Communion with God. The Bread is the Isle of Madascar, and the wine is the Indian (Red) Ocean. To achieve Communion with God, think of the head of Africa as also being your head. The Red Sea represents a creative nerve cell flowing toward Mt. Sinai, where God gave Moses the Ten Commandments, and in your head, in the same general area where you reflect conscious thought. As your life force flows toward Mt. Sinai, your thoughts are divided by the Ten Commandments; which say in part, "You shall not kill." If you obey them, and put on the head of Jesus Christ, through following his word in the Bible, your life force will go to the Holy Land, which is named to represent 'God's Domain', Paradise. Madagascar, the Bread of Communion with God, is like a Jesus washed (purified) foot that will spirit you from Mt. Sinai to Jacob's ladder to heaven, (Genesis 28:10-22), and Zion, the City of God (Psalms 48); to live eternally with the redeemed (John 17). If you disobey the Ten Commandments and Jesus, your life force will go to the left of Mt. Sinai, dug through the Bitter Lakes to be with the Devil. God symbolized him in the left side of Crete, over the head of Africa; and enlarged in the insert. He will make you cry. So, see Communion with God through the 'eyes' of Victoria. Obey the Ten Commandments and the word of Jesus Christ. God's seal makes no allowances for holy or any other kind of wars. His sign is supreme. Jesus cried and died because he truly called himself the Son of God. He was betrayed by a man named Judas. Many years before another man named Judas

Lake Victoria

MADAGASCAR

25th Meridian East

CRETE

was an Israelite hero for the way he beat back the Syrians. His name was changed to Maccabee, or Hammerer; so that by the time of Jesus, Judas was synonymous with Hammerer. Note the hammer mark in the top of the skull. Jesus died at a place called The Skull; named for the shape of the hill on which it happened, symbolically like Africa. This Skull, The Godhead, proves Jesus. Paul said 'we should not be spoiled by philosophy or vain deceit, for in Christ dwells the fullness of the Godhead bodily' (Colossians 2:8-10). Jesus said his meat was to do the will of his Father in heaven. As the Son of man, he 'walked' with God his Father. Note foot shaped Madagascar. Jesus cried for you to follow his foot shaped Bread of Communion, as directed on the map. Obey the Ten Commandments, and 'walk' in Communion with him to the Holy Land, God's Paradise, as you learn about Jesus in church. Be kind, do unto others as you would have them do to you. Send copies of this around the world. 'Walk' in Communion with God, building his kingdom on earth.

INDIAN OCEAN

by Dr. Wayne E. Oakes

CHRIST BECKONS YOU

Christ's head upon our earth
    Cries out to you and me.
In it God has truly shown
    What life should really be.

So hearken to God's holy call;
    Nothing else can compare.
Live for Christ in what you do;
    Help God's people everywhere.

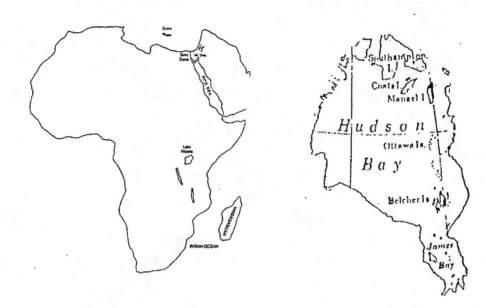

"Copyright permission Hammond
Incorporated, Maplewood, N.J."

CHRIST IN LEFT PUTS COMMANDMENTS RIGHT

Christ sits in left, seen at God's right hand.
  God sits in left, seen from top of world.
God cherishes Christ; doing his work,
  As Commandments go right, where 'Red Sea' is swirled.

Grano had no Lutheran Church;
  So Grandma became Pentecostal.
Reverend Upsetta pastored her.
  God's Upsetta has Communion call.

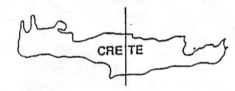

25th Meridian East

Svalbard Map
"Copyright permission Hammond
Incorporated. Maplewood, N.J."

JESUS THE TWENTY-FIFTH

See the lad of Nordoustlandet
    In Norway's 'Northeastland'.
A sideways look for you reveals
    A longhaired pouting head of man.

Determined in his stride,
    Eyeing Helsink I, he stands
With mind at 25th Meridian
    Divides the Devil's bands.

"His disciples said to (Jesus), "Twenty-four prophets have
spoken in Israel, and they all spoke of you." He said to
them, "You have disregarded the living one who is in your
presence, and have spoken of the dead."

Gospel of Thomas 59
Complete Gospels, p. 311

CHRIST'S DIRECTIONS

"(12). The disciples said to Jesus, 'We know that you will depart from us. Who is to be our leader?' Jesus said to them, 'Wherever you are, you are to go to James the righteous, for whose sake heaven and earth came into being.'"

The Gospel of Thomas

"And I say also unto thee, That thou art Peter, and upon this rock I will build my church; and the gates of hell shall not prevail against it. And I will give unto thee the keys of the kingdom of heaven: and whatsoever thou shalt bind on earth shall be bound in heaven: and whatsoever thou shalt loose on earth shall be loosed in heaven."

Matthew 16:18-19

"Copyright permission: Hammond Incorporated, Maplewood, N.J."

ELECT OF CHRIST

James and Peter Christ did choose.
    James was chosen for close accord.
Unite within Christ's church,
    And place their books centerward.

Peter is special to Christ.
    Angel appeared at tomb and said
Tell Peter and the disciples
    To Galilee Christ would tread.

For James, who Christ called righteous,
    Our heaven and earth were made.
So put on head, commune with God;
    James and Hudson Bay your aid.

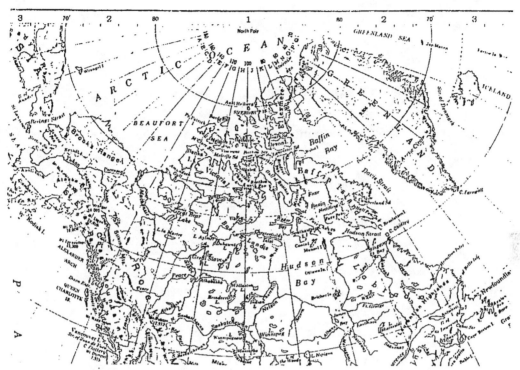

"Copyright permission: Hammond Incorporated, Maplewood, N.J."

JAMES THE HARMONIZER

God the King awaits Communion
    In his watery form his nod.
Put on the head in Southwestern Shore;
    Rise up to Commune with God.

God chose James for his holy head.
    Supplanter is what name means.
James was the brother of Jesus.
    His book God's choice of themes.

God gave judgment to his Son.
    In Africa you've seen it.
Christ's inclusions are in James
    Call from God to live most fit.

COMMANDMENT RIGHT

God's heart is torn in Belcher Isles.
    God belches out his heart, you see,
Through Communion with The Land Across.*
    On the cross Christ cried for thee.

God himself sits in the right
    In James and Hudson Bays.
Communicant is at the left;
    At God's right hand he prays.

God belches out his heart to us,
    And shows his head as 'Book' of James.
God's heart is torn by diverse ways;
    Come together with God's acclaims.

Those who kill for their acclaims
    Do work of Devil in their days.
Reject the Devil, live for Christ;
    Show his right in moral ways.

Rise up, Commune with God.
    Ten Commandments take you right.
Make your life a Godly tune.
    Walk with Christ as your insight.

God made both our left and right
    Work together for common good.
Don't crucify a social conscience;
    Show compassion as Christ would.

*God the King shows his Spiritual Bread of
Communion through Akimiski Isle meaning
The Land Across.

86

MOHAMMED PRAYED
WE LIVE IN PEACE

Oh God, You are peace. From You is peace and to You is peace. Let us live, O Lord, in peace and receive us in Your paradise, the abode of peace. Yours is the majesty and the praise, we hear and we obey. Grant us your forgiveness, Lord, and to you is our becoming.

The Prophet Mohammed CA. 570-632

LIVE GOD'S PLAN

Mohammed said God is peace,
    And prayed for peaceful lives.
So let us strive as we work
    Creating peace for paradise.

Paradise is the eternal home
    Where God's blessed people dwell.
Live God's Plan for holy life;
    Given so life with God we gel.

You cannot war and live God's Plan.
    Christ's head you know as way.
Let U.N. rule through Christ's head,
    So peaceful life comes full sway.

THE MILLENNIUM

The Millennium is said to be
    A period of holiness.
Ten Commandments people obey;
    Walking with Christ in openness.

To walk with Christ is to do his will;
    James best speaks to tell it.
As Christ's brother he knew his thoughts.
    That book of James a retrofit.

God wants all people brought together
    Through signs that tell his Plan.
Coalesce main thoughts of Prophets
    With God's work in earth for man.

Christ to reign and Devil be bound.
    People's days like those of a tree.
Christmas Stocking rides on a colt.
    Peter with keys, you've seen trustee.

The Lord shall establish thee an holy people unto himself, as he
hath sworn unto thee, if thou shalt keep the commandments of the
Lord thy God, and walk in his ways. Deuteronomy 28:29.

Blessed and holy are those who have part in the first
resurrection. The second death has no power over them, but they
will be priests of God and of Christ and will reign with him for
a thousand years. Revelation 20:6.

GOD'S WILL IN MAN

Half of chromosomes are the same
    And other half quite similar
'Tween modern man and chimpanzees.

Structured protein in D.N.A.
    Differs only 'bout one per cent
'Tween modern man and chimpanzees.*

Chimpanzees pass on to young
    Language signs of the deaf.
Voice box in man, not chimpanzees.

Only people working as gods
    Teach reading and writing,
And Godly things to chimpanzees.

Can you question route of God
    Creating highest form of life
Using route of chimpanzees?

God breathed in man his Spirit:*
    Which we proudly claim.
God's will's to man, not chimpanzees.

* Grzimek, Bernard; "Modern Humans", Encyclopedia of Mammals, McGraw Hill, 1990, Vol. II, p. 527.

* James 4:5 refers to God's Spirit he breathed into man. God's Spirit caused man to develop as he did.

CAUSE EARTH TO HUM GOD'S PLAN

God's Spirit's in the elements!
    It replicates and moves;
Causing forms of God's own choosing;
    As Christ's head and James now proves.

Created by God with the power of choice,
    You know the route God tells to take.
God speaks his message through the heads
    He formed fore man was caused to wake.

Pledge to our maker you'll be true.
    You're the reason for God's Plan.
He signed the way for you to live.
    Sing his tune with Godly span.

Government's onus must always be
    To show God's care with material support.
To spread God's Plan and share the wealth,
    So life is hummed with Godly consort.

GOD'S CARE

The signs God made are here to last.
    Don't fear their going out of date.
God speaks out for time to come,
    "My way of life create".

You know our God cares for you;
    'Cause our Father set the stage
For all mankind to worship him.
    Cause Plan of God to be the rage.

God's loving care he's shown for me.
    His form from James and Hudson Bays
Looks down at where I've lived my life,
    And his Light aroused my craze;
So I'd reveal God's Plan for ways.

You know God moved the continents;
    The elements sing his refrain.
This explains how Jesus Christ
    Caused miracles that were germane.
So spread God's Plan to every vein.

Copy poems 'bout signs and way.
    Give them out wherever you go;
Asking others to pass poems on.
    Cause God's love to always grow.

GOD'S LOVE COMMAND

The Bible tells us God is love.
    His love is what he gave
Through Ten Commands, God's grant,
    So life with him we pave.

Bible says Commands are love
    For better life on earth.
Conscience reigns at Sinai
    So lives with God we birth.

Spread God's signs to all
    So earth takes on God's tone;
And life is lived for him
    As happiness is grown.

Christ's Commandment is to love.
    It sums the Godly Ten –
To tread God's holy path
    For life with him, Amen.

RED, WHITE AND BLUE, AND GREEN TOO

Red, red, courage fed;
    Oh how you've bled.
White, white, the resurrection light;
    Christian starred delight.
Blue, blue, God's royal water –
    Loyalty true.
Red, white and blue, and green too;
    Green for Christian growth;
The thing to do!
    Building the kingdom of God.

THE LIBERTY DIME

The Liberty Dime has meaning sure;
　　It's nickel and copper with silver allure.
Its head a resolute Roosevelt brand;
　　'In God We Trust' it chins our stand.

The Freedom Torch of truth and knowledge
　　Is carved on back for you to wedge
Into your light God comforts in;
　　So goals of God may come to win.

To left of 'Torch' is a Tulip Tree;
　　Its issues coned for you to see.
With social conscience let truth prevail;
　　The Freedom Torch for you to hail.

To right of 'Torch' an Oak stands bold;
　　Its fruit the word believers mold.
In God it trusts that all will stand
　　For goals to keep our country grand.

PSALM 100

Make a joyful noise unto the Lord,
   all ye lands.
Serve the Lord with gladness: come
   before his presence with singing.
Know ye that the Lord he is God: it
   is he that hath made us, and not we
   ourselves, we are his people, and
   the sheep of his pasture.
Enter into his gates with thanksgiving,
   and into his courts with praise: be
   thankful unto him, and bless his
   name.
For the Lord is good; his mercy is
   everlasting; and his truth endureth
   to all generations.

GOD'S SPIRIT PLAN

To this I know and testify:
    God came to me as Light.
He claimed my inner soul
    Affecting me to write.

In James and Hudson Bays
    The water shows his form.
His vital fluid of all life
    With Light of his we're born.

God's Spirit shapes this Isle of Man.
    Ireland shows God's Spirit's here;
And Kathy's spirit entered it
    As her car rolled severe.

Then back to life she came,
    And she did testify
Of dimension of the Spirit.
    God planned our Spirit ply.

God's Spirit moves the earth;
    His desire shaped in Plan.
Africa's form shows his will;
    So walk with Christ to span.

His dimension need to seek;
    Ten Commands are his cue.
Then when life we know is done
    God's Spirit waits for you.

If God's Spirit comes to earth,
    God's Spirit sure can go
To other worlds of our God
    Where he commands the show.

God caused me to have experiences that prove him through the messages he imprinted on the world before he created mankind. With the billions of people there are on the earth today, in his planning God caused them to be important to salvation, or he would not have spent the time to form the world as he did in our time. Because of the different religions, and those who say there is no proof of God, there needs to be an era of enlightenment. Marx debated against God, not realizing the choices imprinted in the head of Africa. Ron Barker left the ministry and joined the Freedom from Religion Council, an atheistic group, because of his doubts; and there are others. There is no denying the proof that God himself developed in the earth. The Bible says there will be signs. I have simply revealed them. This is not a new religion. Jesus Christ is still supreme. These signs comfort him.

I dedicate this writing to my wife Elva Jean; our son Jon Sherman and his wife Lisa; her children Neil and Brycelyn; to Jon's daughter Aryn Rebecca and to her husband Craig Anderton, and to their children Hannah Rose, Coleman Garrett, Emma Kate and Gwen Elizabeth; and Jon's other daughter Cara Susan, and her children Claire Abigail and Alison Camille; to our son Robert Jacob, and his wife Charlene and their son Chad Robert; to our son Gerald DuWayne; our dsughter Kathleen Ann Failey, and her children Jacob Christopher and Sarah Christine; to our daughter Mary Jean, her husband Martin James Mitts, and to their children Jared Martin and his wife Claudette, Jordan DuWayne Scott, and Anna Christine; my parents Ralph William Oakes and Ella Catherine Anderson; my sister Beverly Ann and her husband Robert E. Lee, and their family; my sister Diana Lee and her husband Gary Vick and their family; my wife's parents Jacob and Elfrieda Adeline Jacobson; my wife's sister June Elaine and her husband Paul Stratton, and their family; and her sister Evelyn Kathlene and her husband Morris Jack Turner, and their family; and my friends and all seekers of God's truths.

My friends Dr. Calvin Watness, his brother Rev. Col. Luther Watness, and Rev. Frank Brocker, read my original manuscript at various stages of my writing. I have sent different writings to other people since the mid 1970's. Calvin referred to it as being, "quite an epistle." His brother Luther said proof of my experiences is verified in what God caused me to reveal. Joyce Weaver thought of my experiences and writings as being my reason for living. Early in my writing, Dr. Richard Moe said he could understand why God formed the head of Africa as he did. Rev. Edward Larson pondered the influence my writings would have in the future. My friend Daniel Grefthen asked what does it tell us to do? I emphasize obey the Ten Commandments and Commune with Christ, building the Kingdom of God as you pray in The Lord's Prayer.

I pray this writing is as meaningful as God intended. You are his highest form of creation, created in his image. He wants all people on earth to live caring, peaceful lives. He planned for you from the beginning.

Poems titled A Peek at God's Signs and Jesus the Way
are on display in the International Society of Poets Hall of
Fame Museum. You may see them on the web at:
     http://.poets.com/DuWayneOakes.html
Copy these poems and help God through giving them to others.

     Undesignated maps are public domain.

BIBLIOGRAPHY

The Complete Gospels, Robert J. Miller, Editor,
Polbridge Press, Sonoma, 1992.

The Nag Hammadi Library in English, Third, Completely
Revised Edition, James M. Robinson, General Editor, Harpor and
Row, San Francisco, 1988.

The New Analytical Bible and Dictionary of the Bible,
Authorized King James Version, Comprehensive Subject Index
Edition, (Chicago: John A. Dickson Publishing Company, c.
1929).

Grzimek, Bernard; "Modern Humans", Encyclopedia of
Mammals, McGraw Hill, 1990, Vol. II, p. 527.